For Rob, Skyler, and Luca.—K. S.

To my children, Sidsel Emilie,
Gabriel, and Rumle Michael.—M. E.

ALIEN TOMATO

Kristen Schroeder

illustrated by Mette Engell

PAGE
STREET
KIDS

It streaked through the sky
on a perfect day in July…

and landed in the garden.

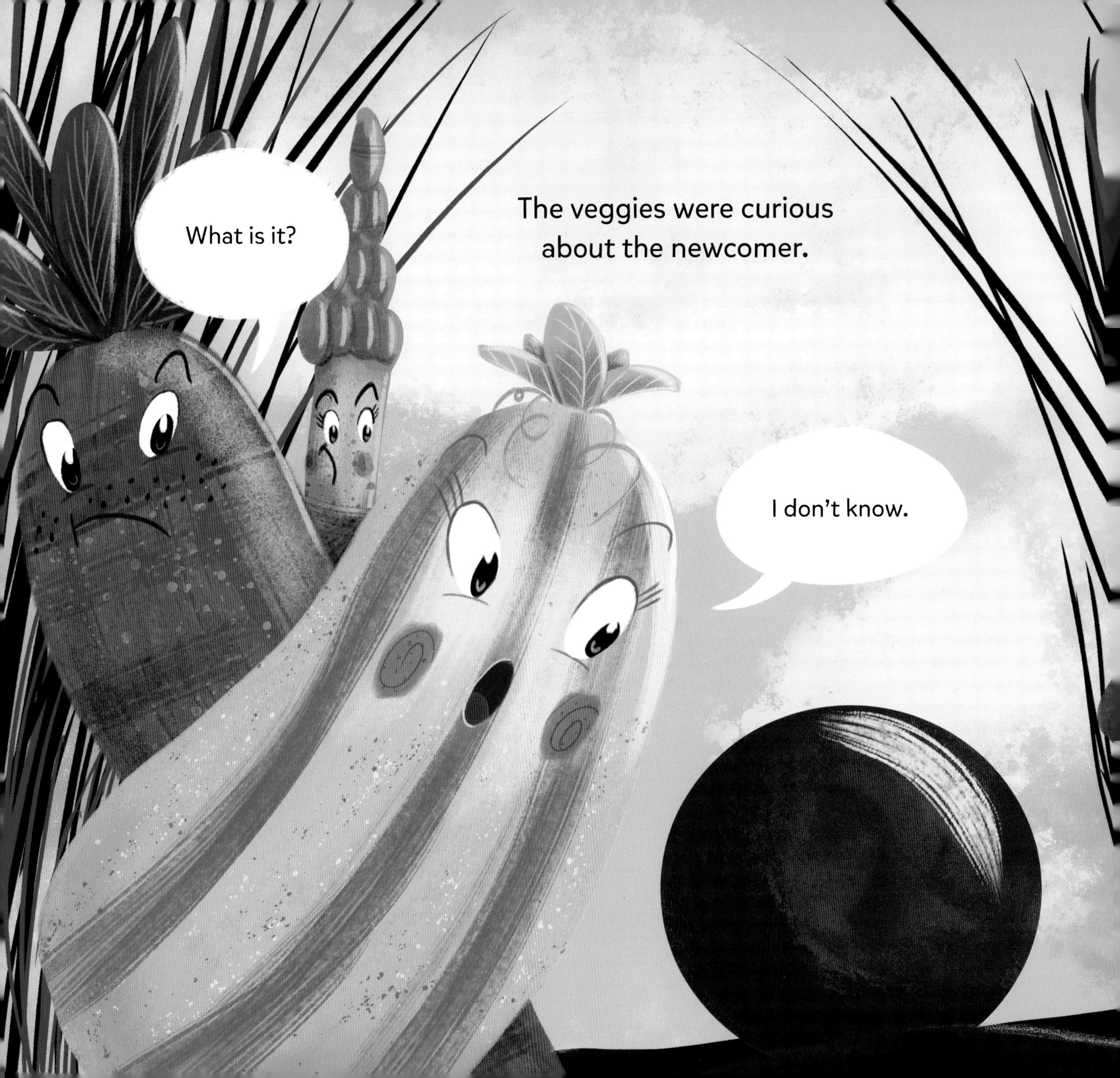

The veggies were curious about the newcomer.

They shared their ideas.

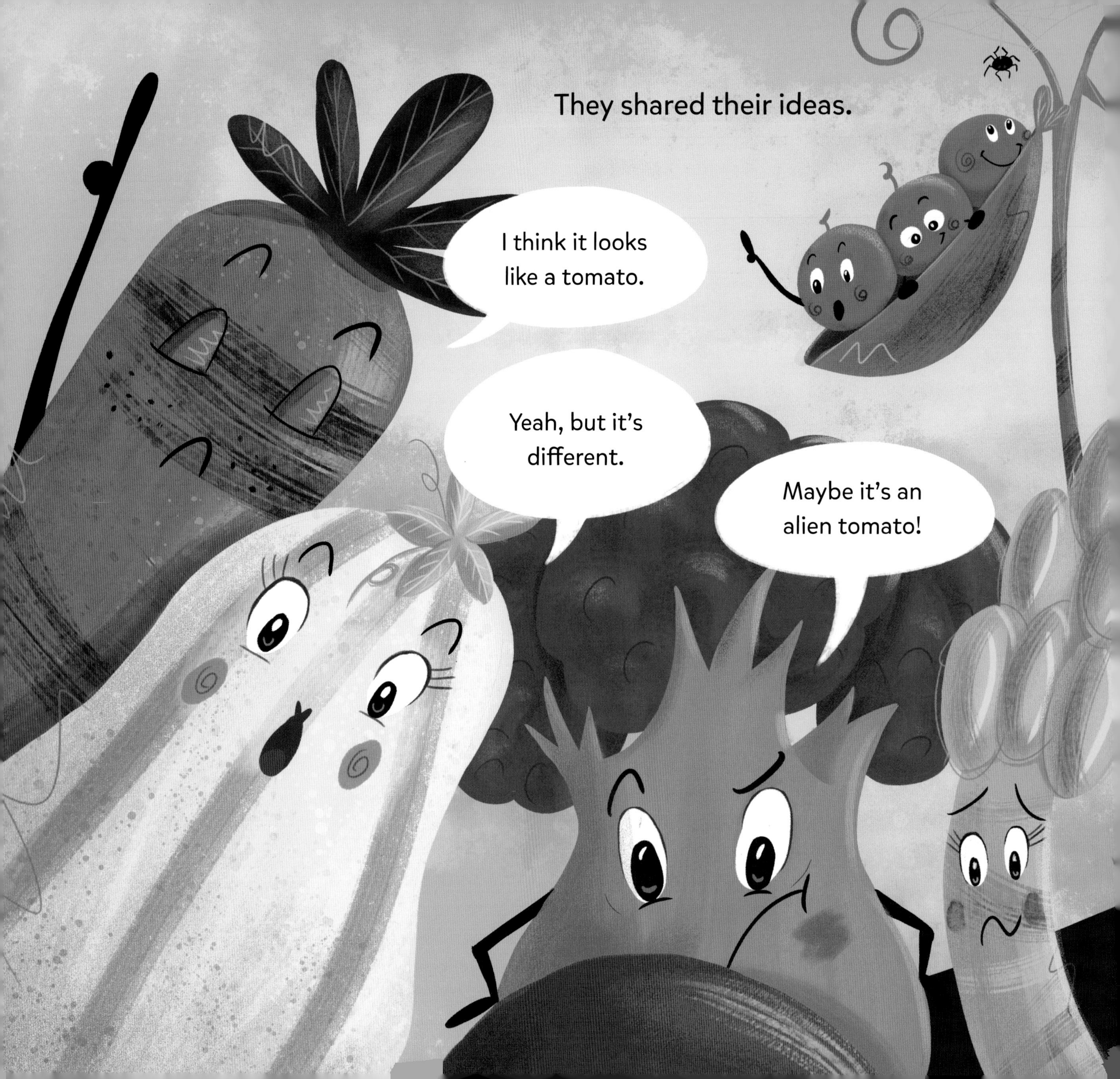

But the veggies didn't know anything about alien tomatoes.

They decided a friendly approach was best.

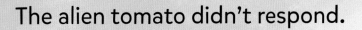

The alien tomato didn't respond.

They decided to throw Allie a welcome party.

Nobody ever held a party for ME.

And treated her like an honored guest.

A crown? Really?
This is getting ridiculous!

The veggies enjoyed spending time with Allie.
They were all on their best behavior.

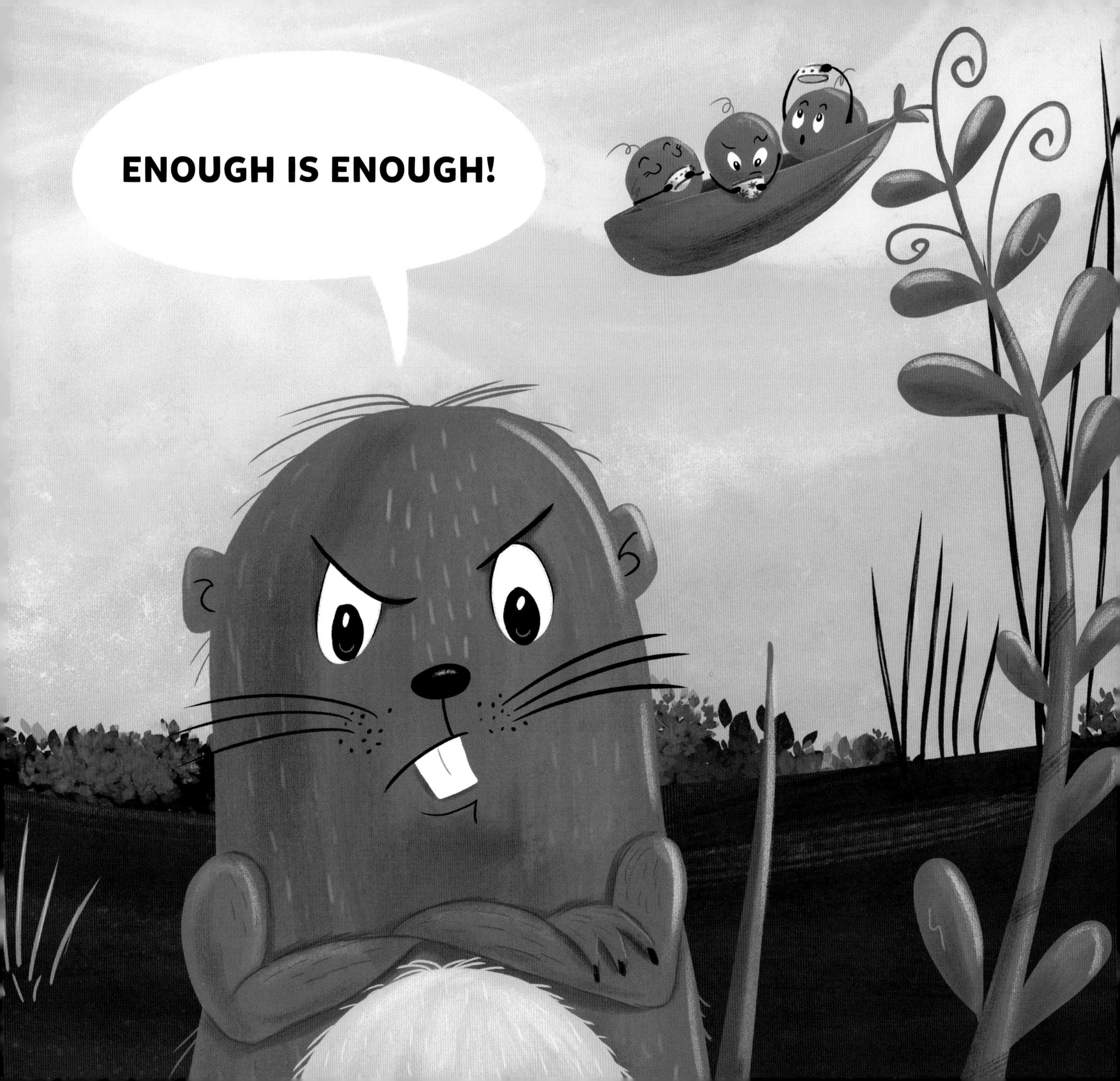
ENOUGH IS ENOUGH!

But then, strange things happened while the veggies slept.

Allie turned up in the far corner of the garden, and her crown disappeared.

What's wrong, Allie?

Do you need more shade?

More water?

Everyone agreed. Allie must have gone back to her own planet.

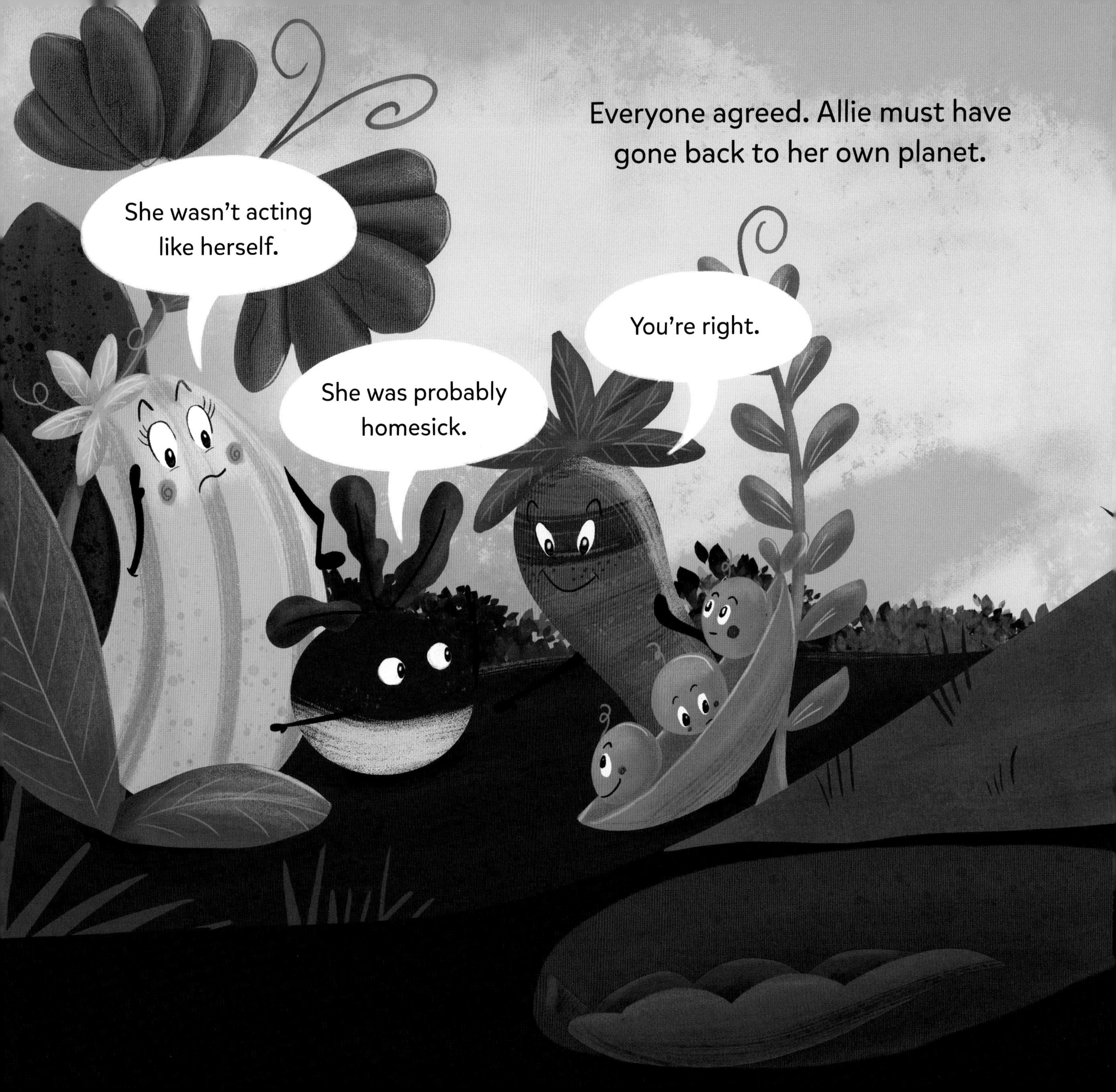

They all missed her.

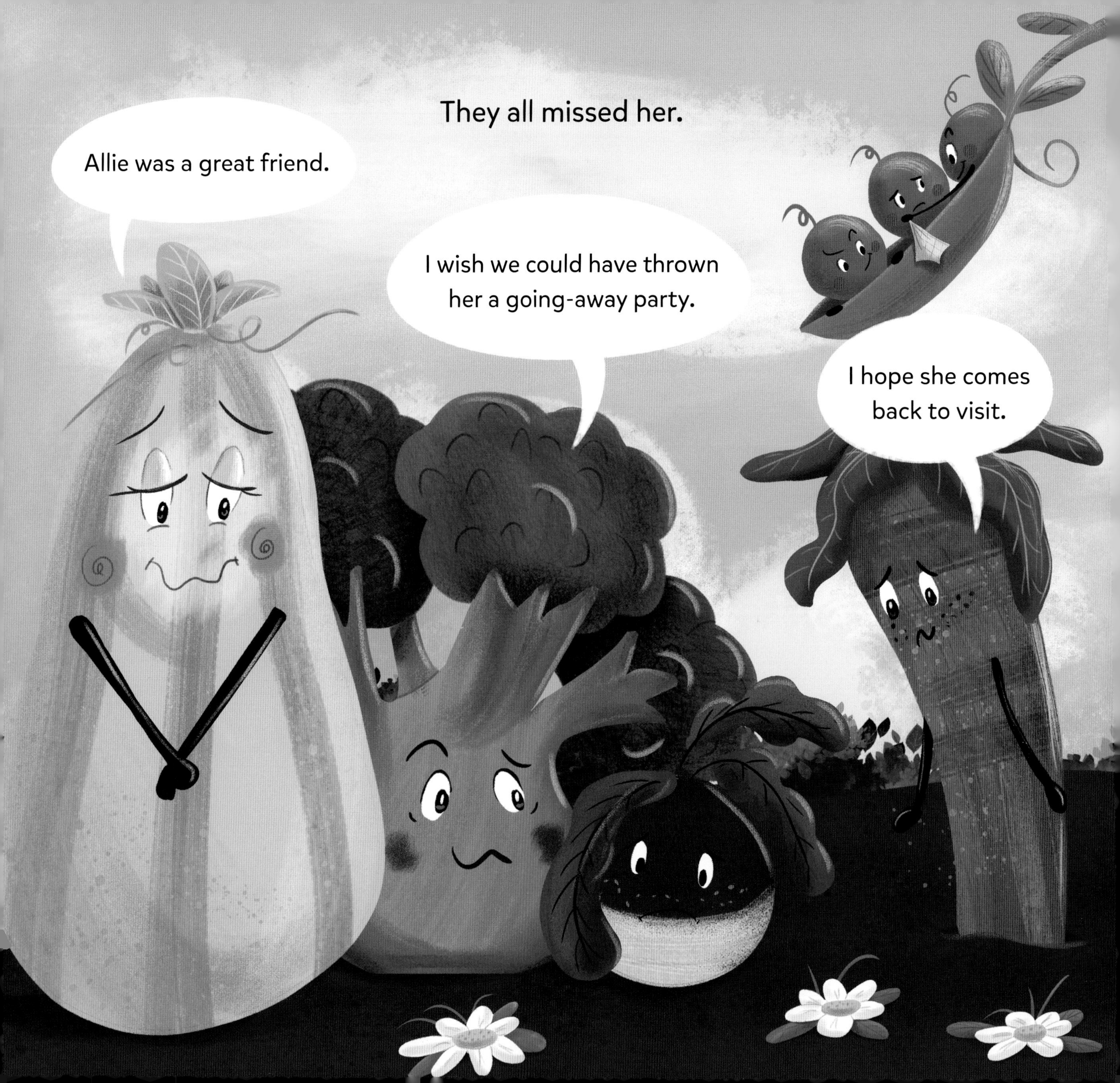

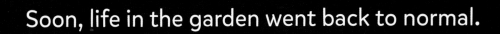

Soon, life in the garden went back to normal.

Allie...

Until something streaked through the sky on a starry night in August.